Ice-Skating Rescue

Story by Annette Smith
Illustrations by Lidia Fernández Abril

Contents

Chapter 1

Getting Ready

It was the first morning of the winter school holidays. Jin, Lee and their parents had arrived the previous night at a lodge below some snow-covered mountains.

"Wake up, Lee," called Jin. "Today is going to be a great day for ice skating."

Lee rolled over and peered out the window beside his bunk. "It's been snowing during the night," he said. "The lake should be frozen solid."

"I hope so," replied Jin, "because I want to try out some speed skating."

"You know you won't beat Mum and Dad," said Lee.

"Just wait and see, little brother," said Jin, grinning.

After breakfast, the boys helped Dad pack the truck with extra jackets and some food supplies.

"I'll check my toolbox for tow ropes and chains for the tyres," said Dad. "If the road is icy we don't want to be stranded up there on the mountain."

"I've called the mountain park rangers to let them know we will be up at Rainbow Lake," said Mum, coming out of the lodge. "They've told me the lake is frozen, but we must remember there's no mobile phone coverage in that area."

"We'll be careful," said Lee. "Come on. Let's go before there are too many people at the lake. I need plenty of space to try out my new skating tricks."

Chapter 2

Disaster Strikes

Mum parked the truck at the car park, some distance from the lake.

The boys were out of the truck at once. They ran off ahead, up a winding track on the hill, and through some snow-covered rocks and trees.

"These new skates are fantastic," said Lee, as he tightened the laces. "I'm sure I'll be able to race you, Jin. Are you ready for a challenge?"

"Of course I'm ready," said Jin, laughing and gliding out onto the ice. "This year *I'm* going to be the speed-skating champ in the family!"

Mum and Dad watched the boys as they raced around the edge of the frozen lake. The sun glistened on the snow, and long icicles hung from the trees.

"This is such a beautiful place," said Mum. "It's perfect for ice skating. Let's get ready, too."

"Did I hear someone say that *he* was going to be this family's speed-skating champ?" called Dad, as the boys swerved towards him and Mum. "Surely you've heard of 'Joe … the Silver Blade Speedster'."

"Oh, Dad, you're not going to tell us *that* story again," groaned Jin. "We all know that Mum is the best skater in the family. She has won all the competitions she's entered for years."

"Yeah," said Lee. "Look at her. She can do all sorts of cool tricks, and they're much harder to do than speed skating."

Jin, Lee and Dad watched as Mum whirled and twirled effortlessly around the lake.

"I can show you a few fancy tricks, too," said Dad, "but I'll have to get a bit of speed up first."

Dad raced across the lake, bending low as he gathered speed. It wasn't long before he had completed a lap around the lake.

All of a sudden, he lost his balance. His legs flew into the air and he landed with a thud on the ice.

“That’s a good trick, Dad,” called Jin, laughing as everyone skated over to Dad.

“I don’t know about that,” Dad replied, wincing with pain. “I’ve hurt my ankle. Can you help me over to the edge of the ice, please? This could be the end of my tricks for the day.”

Mum helped Dad take off his skate.

“Look at my ankle!” said Dad. “It’s starting to swell already, but it feels as though it could just be a sprain.”

“I hope it’s not broken,” said Lee, looking at Dad anxiously.

Mum skated over to her backpack and took out a small towel. "I'll use this to pack some snow around your ankle," she said to Dad. "It should help stop the swelling. But we're going to have to think of some way to get you back down to the truck. It's too far for you to hobble."

"That feels a bit better," said Dad, holding the towel firmly against his ankle. "Maybe I should try to stand and see if I can walk around."

"No!" said Mum. "You could do more damage to your ankle. We need to get you down the track to the truck, so I can drive you to the hospital."

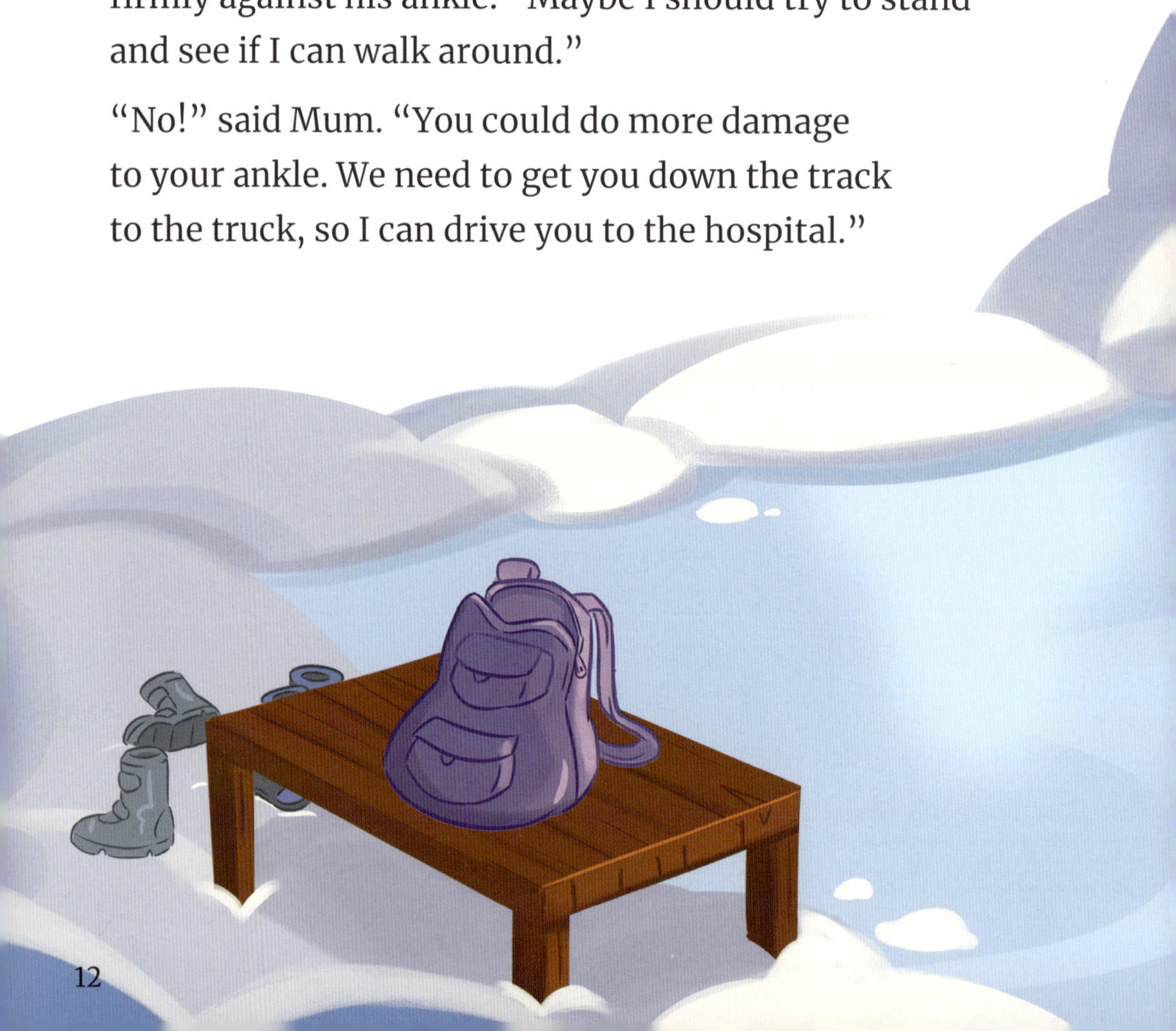

Chapter 3

A Great Idea

"Mum," said Lee, "let's call the mountain park rangers. They might bring a helicopter up here and fly Dad to the hospital. That would be exciting!"

"Oh, Lee!" said Jin, looking around at the icy, snow-covered track. "They wouldn't bring a helicopter up here. There are too many trees."

"The mountain rangers could help carry Dad back to the truck," Mum said. "But I would need to drive down the mountain to call them. It would be several hours before I got back."

"Why don't we make a sled for Dad," said Lee, "and then we could slide him down to the truck."

"Hey!" said Jin. "You're right. We can use the lid of the toolbox! Come on, Lee. I'll need your help. Put on your snow boots and come back to the truck with me."

"That's a great idea," said Mum. "I'll stay here with Dad."

"Don't move," Lee told Dad. "We won't be long."

Soon, Jin and Lee returned from the truck. They were carrying some of the tow ropes and the large lid from the toolbox.

"Dad," said Lee, "we're going to make you the best sled you've ever seen!"

“A sled is just what I need,” said Dad with a laugh. “This might be more fun than skating!”

The boys got to work tying the ropes to one of the handles of the big toolbox lid. Mum helped Dad get onto it.

"Lee and I will pull from the front until we get you to the top of the hill," said Jin.
"Mum, we're going to need you to push."

"And I'll support my ankle," said Dad.
"This is going to be real teamwork."

The boys took hold of the ropes.

"Right, everyone, let's go!" called Jin.

Chapter 4

The Rescue in Action

Mum and the boys slipped and slid over the icy ground as they hauled Dad up to the top of the hill.
At last they could see the truck through the trees.
It was parked on the road far below.

"That was hard work," said Lee, puffing.
"I hope the next bit is easier."

"It won't be," said Jin. "We have to get Dad down that steep slope without tipping him off the sled."

Jin, Lee and Mum carefully untied the ropes from the front of the sled and tied them onto the back. Dad looked down the hill towards the car park.

"If I move my weight from side to side," said Dad, "then I can help steer it."

"Are you ready, Joe?" laughed Mum. "Hold on tight! This is one race you're definitely going to win, as we'll all be behind you!"

The toolbox lid began to move down the slope – slowly at first, but then it gathered speed.

"Slow this thing down!" yelled Dad. "Remember, I can't steer it properly, and I don't want two sprained ankles."

Mum, Jin and Lee were laughing so much that they could hardly pull on the ropes at the back.

Dad huddled forward, holding his ankle
and steering the lid at the same time.
The lid swerved towards a large tree,
but he managed to stop it in a snowdrift, just in time.

At last they reached the bottom of the slope
and Mum, Jin and Lee helped Dad into the truck.

"The toolbox lid made a great sled," said Dad. "That was smart thinking, boys."

"We'll have lots of fun using it again next time we come to Rainbow Lake," said Lee.

"I've had plenty of sledding practice today, thanks," said Dad with a grin. "I guess that makes me the sledding champion of the family!"